EIGHT ANIMALS PLAY BALL

By **Susan Middleton Elya**

Illustrated by **Lee Chapman**

G. P. Putnam's Sons

PITCHER   CATCHER

To all the great people who take time to coach kids' sports.
—S.M.E.

To my dogs, Albert, Nellie, and Frida, who love to play ball!
—L. C.

THIRD BASE   REFEREE   BATTER

Glossary and Pronunciation Guide

Abrigos (ah BREE goce) coats
Alas (AH lahs) wings
Amigos (ah MEE goce) friends
Animales (ah nee MAH lehs) animals
Árbitro (AHR bee troe) referee
Bate (BAH teh) bat
Béisbol (BEHS bole) baseball
Boliche (boe LEE cheh) bowling
Bueno (BWEH noe) good
Caballo (kah BAH yoe) horse
Cerdo (SEHR doe) pig
Cometa (koe MEH tah) kite
Eh, Bateador (EH, bah teh ah DOHR)
   hey, Batter
Estrái (ehs TRY) strike
Fútbol (FUTE bole) soccer
Fútbol americano (FUTE bole
   ah meh ree KAH noe) football
Gato (GAH toe) cat
Heno (EH noe) hay

Jonrón (hone RONE) home run
Lanzador (lahn sah DOHR) pitcher
Lluvia (YOO vee ah) rain
Ocho (OH choe) eight
Olé (oh LEH) bravo
Pájaro (PAH hah roe) bird
Parque (PAHR keh) park
Patines de ruedas (pah TEE nehs DEH
   RWEH dahs) roller skates
Perro (PEH rroe) dog
Rana (RRAH nah) frog
Ratón (rrah TONE) mouse
*Silbato (seel BAH toe) whistle
Soy mejor (SOY meh HORE) I'm better
Vaca (VAH kah) cow
Zapatos de tenis (sah PAH toce DEH
   TEH neece) sneakers/tennis shoes

*In proper Spanish, **Vaca**'s **silbato** would be
written **silbato de Vaca**.

CABALLO THE HORSE — OUTFIELD

PERRO THE DOG — FIRST BASE

PÁJARO THE BIRD — SECOND BASE

Eight **animales**, ready to play,
head for the **parque**—the park—
for the day.

Mouse comes with roller skates strapped to his feet.
"**Patines de ruedas**," **Ratón** says, "are neat."
"I need to practice my batting," says Cat.
Gato brings a **bate**, her special new bat.

SNEAKERS = ZAPATOS de TENIS

Next to show up, wearing sneakers, is Dog—
zapatos de tenis so **Perro** can jog.

KITE=COMETA

Bird comes by next with a colorful kite.
"**Cometa**," says **Pájaro**, "ready for flight."

Frog wants to bowl, so he brings ball and shoes.
"**Boliche**," says **Rana**, "a game I can't lose."
Horse kicks a soccer ball into a net.
Caballo says, "**Fútbol**—the greatest sport yet."

Cow brings a whistle and wears black and white.
"A **silbato**," says **Vaca**, "so none of you fight."

Pig has a football tucked under his arm. **"Fútbol americano,"** says **Cerdo**, "has charm!"

Eight **animales** now have to choose
which game to play, which equipment to use.
Perro says, "No one can skate but **Ratón**.
It's not so much fun if you do it alone."

Cerdo says,
"**Rana** can't bowl at the park,
and **Caballo** is guarding
his ball like a shark."

Gato says, "I'll share my **bate** and play
a good game of baseball." **Ratón** shouts, "¡Olé!"
"Our coats will be bases, and I'm first at bat.
Vaca will ref in her **árbitro** hat!"

Gato warms up, and three more take a base.
Ratón slides a catcher's mask over his face.

Cerdo sniffs second base, **Pájaro**'s coat.
Caballo says, "¿**Béisbol**? Don't I get to vote?"

Rana winds up. **Vaca**'s nose starts to twitch.
"Ball!" she declares as she judges the pitch.

Next is a curveball, so **Gato** swings low.
"¡**Estrái**!" **Vaca** yells. Cat has two strikes to go.

The game's going well now, and everything's **bueno**.
Caballo plays outfield while munching on **heno**.

Rana's next pitch is the best one he's thrown.
So **Gato** crack-whacks it and hits a **jonrón**.
"A homer!" says **Gato**. "I've scored the first run!"
But **Caballo** gets angry. He's done having fun.

"I'm better at batting than you! ¡**Soy mejor**!"
He waits for the pitch from the green **lanzador**.

He swings; it connects! He pop-whops it to first!
But **Perro** is ready, as though he rehearsed.
He catches the pop-up. **Caballo** is out!
He goes to play outfield. He's starting to pout.

"Batter up!" **Vaca** orders.
Now **Cerdo** is batter.

The others play infield
and practice their chatter.
"Hey, Batter, Batter! ¡Eh, **Bateador**!
Why, you couldn't hit
this next ball with a door!"

So **Cerdo** quits playing.
His feelings are hurt.
He stomps off the field,
and he kicks at the dirt.
The game's going sour;
it's no fun anymore.
Big rain clouds are forming.
It soon starts to pour!

While **Pájaro** spreads out her **alas**—her wings—
the other ones hurry to snatch up their things.

Caballo shares coats with both **Perro** and **Gato**.
And **Cerdo** trades his coat for **Vaca**'s **silbato**.

Eight **animales**,
out in the weather,
bickering finished,
just glad they're together.
Cozy and dry under wings and **abrigos**,
they're eight drip-dry friends.
That's **ocho amigos**.

Published simultaneously in Canada. Manufactured in China by South China Printing Co. (1988) Ltd.
Designed by Carolyn T. Fucile. Text set in Pacific Clipper Medium. The art was done in oil pastel on paper.
Library of Congress Cataloging-in-Publication Data   Elya, Susan Middleton, 1955– Eight animals play ball /
by Susan Middleton Elya; illustrated by Lee Chapman.   p.   cm.   Summary: Eight animal friends play baseball in the
park. Includes words in Spanish.   [1. Parks—Fiction. 2. Baseball—Fiction. 3. Friendship—Fiction. 4. Animals—Fiction.
5. Stories in rhyme.] I. Chapman, Lee, ill. II. Title.   PZ8.3.E514 Ek 2003   [E]—dc21   2001048249
ISBN 0-399-23569-8
1 3 5 7 9 10 8 6 4 2
First Impression